THE LAST
OF THE
ENDER CRYSTAL

THE LAST
OF THE
ENDER CRYSTAL

AN UNOFFICIAL OVERWORLD HEROES ADVENTURE, BOOK FIVE

DANICA DAVIDSON

Sky Pony Press
New York

10 9 8 7 6 5 4 3 2 1

Library of Congress Cataloging-in-Publication Data is available on file.

Cover design by Brian Peterson
Cover photo by Lordwhitebear

Hardcover ISBN: 978-1-5107-3352-7
Paperback ISBN: 978-1-5107-3351-0
Ebook ISBN: 978-1-5107-3353-4

Printed in the United States of America

THE LAST
OF THE
ENDER CRYSTAL

CHAPTER 1

THE ENDER DRAGON WAS ABOUT TO ESCAPE FROM her prison. I could feel it all the way down to my bones, like a cold wind. The monsters in the land had been growing stronger for weeks, and the nights had gotten so long we barely saw the sun anymore.

Then there was her voice: it kept taunting me, inside my head, promising to do evil deeds if I didn't bow to her. The Overworld's only hope was to find the last crystal shard that my ancestor Steve Alexander had hidden. With it, we could create the ultimate weapon to defeat her.

But we had hit a dead end.

"Read it again," my cousin Alex demanded.

I sighed and read the newest passage we'd decoded in Steve Alexander's enchanted book. We'd already read it a dozen times. After each new crystal we found, the enchantment in the book let us read a little more of the text—but this clue was way too vague. So far Steve Alexander had also been giving us maps in the book to find the next crystal, but we'd gotten no map with this one. And time was running out!

"*For its safety, the final crystal shard has been taken from this world and given to Maya,*" I read. "*Seek out the earth woman.* Alex, that's all it says."

"This is just great," muttered Yancy sarcastically, raking his hand through his dark hair. "We have no map, and apparently this crystal is floating around somewhere on Earth. A tiny little planet which, according to the Internet, has a radius of a mere 3,959 miles. You know, just a quick stroll."

"It's almost like Steve Alexander doesn't want us to find the last crystal shard," murmured Destiny, nervously biting at her fingernails.

"I don't think that's it," Maison argued. She was my best friend, and the first person I had met from Earth. Right now we were all sitting in her bedroom, near her computer, which acted as her portal to the Overworld. Or "*Minecraft,*" as people on Earth called it. "Whenever Steve Alexander gets vague about things, he usually wants us to dig deeper."

"Yeah, and I'm digging," Yancy said, clicking on his phone. Blue, the pet parrot he had tamed in the jungle biome, was perched on Yancy's shoulder, happily chirping. At least that bird was unaware of the stress the rest of us were feeling.

"If we can't track down the crystal, you'd think we'd at least be able to track down Maya, the Earth woman who helped Steve Alexander imprison the Ender Dragon in the first place," he went on. "But you know what the problem is with that? Well, there's the fact that she apparently lived thousands of years ago, before most human cultures had writing systems. Second, when I Googled the name 'Maya,' I got about a million hits. It showed up in all sorts of ancient cultures, not to mention modern ones, so we can't even narrow down where she might have lived. That's not even counting all the cultures that have disappeared over time, so we don't even have records of the names they used."

I'd never thought of cultures disappearing. Was that like how we'd find old, forgotten temples in the Overworld and have no idea who'd made them? It hadn't occurred to me that Earth might have that, too.

"What does all that mean?" I asked.

"It means," Yancy said, "that Steve Alexander is no help on this one. We're down to the last crystal shard, and he's bailed on us. And after all that talk about being a hero. What a loser."

Alex jumped up, furious. "Steve Alexander is the greatest hero the Overworld has ever seen, and he's our great-great-great-whatever grandfather! Don't you be talking about him like that!"

"Fine," Yancy said, tossing his cell phone to Alex. "Then you find the crystal shard, and Maya."

Alex frowned. "I don't know how to use this contraption!"

Alex and I were from the Overworld, while Maison, Destiny, and Yancy all came from Earth. Alex and I knew how to make our own food and build our own homes and create our own weapons. Maison, Destiny, and Yancy knew how to use cell phones and computers and the Internet. We came from very different worlds, but we were still friends.

We were also all part of the Overworld Heroes task force, which had been created by my aunt, Mayor Alexandra. It was supposed to be our mission to stop the Ender Dragon from escaping from the End. The dragon had been threatening to escape for a while, and if she did, her first mission would be to take over the Overworld and go after Steve Alexander's descendants. That meant Alex, Aunt Alexandra, Dad, and me. She hated Steve Alexander for locking her in the End thousands of years ago, and she'd been biding her time, waiting for revenge, ever since.

I ran the crystal over the book's pages. Normally using the newest crystal shard would light up more words so we could read farther. But all these pages were blank. And they stayed blank, crystal or no crystal.

"I think we'll probably have better luck using the original tools Steve Alexander gave us, instead of using the Internet," Maison said quietly. She had been acting really thoughtful while the rest of us were panicking.

"They wouldn't have had the Internet back then, so he and Maya wouldn't have put clues there."

"See? This thing has no answers." Alex threw the phone back at Yancy, and he caught it as it struck him in the chest. "You people on Earth have all these things that are supposed to make your lives easier," Alex said, "but they don't answer the hard questions!"

"Hey, at least we live in a world that isn't overrun with monsters every night," Yancy shot back. Unlike Earth, darkness in the Overworld brought with it an onslaught of zombies; giant, red-eyed spiders; armed skeletons; creepers; and other monsters we called "mobs." Yancy continued, "Maybe if you had more technology, you would have figured out how to get rid of them by now."

Alex's face turned so red it looked like she was about to spit lava. When she opened her mouth to yell something at Yancy, I turned away and tried to clear my thoughts. I knew they were only fighting because they were stressed, but it wasn't going to do any good. Destiny looked miserable and hopeless, while Maison was staring out the window at the cold, rainy day, her mind clearly far away. I went to sit next to Maison.

While Yancy and Alex were arguing, I kept remembering what Yancy had said about Steve Alexander: *What a loser.*

Was he right? Everyone in the Overworld honored Steve Alexander's name, but when you looked at Steve Alexander's own writing, it often sounded like he didn't think he was so heroic. And the Ender Dragon kept hinting that the Steve Alexander we thought we knew wasn't the real Steve Alexander. Then again, she was always lying and manipulating and trying to destroy worlds. Steve Alexander wanted to *save* worlds.

Except now he'd left us stranded. It wasn't fair. Why would he even give us such a weak clue?

"What do you think?" I asked Maison.

"Maya can't be alive anymore, so it's not like we can seek her out," Maison said. "And that must be who he means by 'the Earth woman.'" She thought for another moment. "Unless . . ."

That "unless" was enough to get my heart pounding. Right then, *any* idea was enough to get my heart pounding.

My thoughts were interrupted by a screaming sound.

CHAPTER 2

MAISON GRABBED HER PHONE AND AN-
swered it, cutting off the shrill noise. It had
still made me jump out of my skin. Earth's
technology was always making different sounds. In
the Overworld, only living things made noises, so
if you heard a sound, you knew immediately that a
friend or foe was right by you. Earth was so noisy I
didn't know how the people who lived there full-time
could stand it.

"Hello?" Maison said, distracted. Yancy and Alex
had both stopped arguing for Maison's sake, though
Yancy was eyeing Alex with annoyance and Alex was
glaring at him.

"Oh, hi, Grandma," Maison said. "Yeah, I'm fine,
just busy . . . Yeah, I really can't talk right now . . .
I'll call you back . . . What's that? Oh, thanks. No, I
didn't get your birthday package yet . . . Yeah, I know

turning twelve is a big deal . . . What do you mean, especially in our family? . . . It's a surprise? Okay, okay, Grandma, we'll talk more soon. Love you. Bye."

She hung up, looking a little guilty for rushing her grandma off the phone.

"I forgot your birthday was coming up!" Destiny said. She stopped biting her fingernails for a moment, as though glad to be distracted by something in the real world. "It's this Saturday, right? Are you having a party?"

My mind had been completely elsewhere, too. "It's your birthday?" I said, stunned. It was still a few months before I turned twelve, and Maison had never mentioned her birthday. I didn't want to admit it, but I felt kind of hurt. I thought best friends told each other everything. Were there other things I didn't know about Maison?

"Yeah, it's my birthday this Saturday," Maison said. "But it's not a big deal. This is more important now. I was going to plan a party, except . . ."

"We'll have a big party after we defeat the Ender Dragon!" Destiny promised. Blue whistled excitedly. Destiny sounded eager to talk about something besides the dragon. But Maison was right; we needed to think about the next crystal.

Still, a voice in the back of my head wondered what I should give Maison for her birthday. On Earth people usually bought gifts, but I wanted to make her something, so she'd know it was special.

Trying to get over the fact that Maison hadn't told me this important thing about her life, I asked, "But what were you starting to say before the phone rang? 'Unless' . . . ?"

"It's probably nothing," Maison said. "I just noticed Maya is named in the first sentence, and in the second sentence it says 'Earth woman.' Maybe that 'Earth woman' isn't Maya."

"Who else would it be?" Yancy demanded. "If it's every Earth woman, that would be too easy. And he says 'woman,' not 'women.' I think there's only one person who can help us."

I figured Yancy was probably right. Destiny said, "I still think it's worth a try." She gently took the book from me and moved the crystal over it.

"Nothing," Yancy grunted darkly. "Just like I expected."

"Let me try," Maison said, reaching out.

Yancy rolled his eyes and turned away. "I think we're just wasting time here," he mumbled, crossing his arms.

But he turned back around when he heard a gasp.

As Maison moved the crystal over the next blank page, something began to happen. A purple glow came out of the paper, lighting up the whole room. The violet tint fell all over our shocked faces as we huddled close to see what was going on. No words were coming out of the book, and no map either. No, this was different. A *picture* was forming on the page.

"It's Steve Alexander," I whispered, hardly daring to breathe. Under the crystal in Maison's hand, Steve Alexander's features became clearer and clearer. His legs were spread as if he were riding a horse, and he was holding his diamond sword up. His mouth was open as if shouting a battle cry. He looked totally in his element, strong and determined. This man was no loser, I wanted to tell Yancy.

The details of the picture continued to fill in, like spilled ink slowly making its way to the edges of the illustration. He was definitely riding some sort of animal, but as the picture emerged, I saw the animal was way too big to be a horse. I was confused. I remembered Steve Alexander writing about riding his steed into battle, and I knew "steed" was a fancy word for horse. Then some words spread across the page—a caption reading STEVE ALEXANDER AND HIS BELOVED STEED. So that had to be it.

But when the picture was finished and the details were done shifting, I felt my heart almost stop for a moment. I started to tremble. Everything I knew about the Overworld, everything I believed about Steve Alexander and the Ender Dragon—it all went out the window when I saw that drawing.

"No," I said, feeling all the blood drain from my face. "No, this can't be right! Please tell me this isn't right!" We had been lied to—for thousands and thousands of years, we had been fed nothing but myths!

CHAPTER 3

"**S**TEVIE, GET AHOLD OF YOURSELF," YANCY SAID, putting a steadying hand on my shoulder. I shook him off, unable to look away from the image.

"But look at it!" I said shrilly. "Look!"

It was an image of Steve Alexander.

Riding the Ender Dragon.

His steed!

"That's not right," I said. "They're mortal enemies. Steve Alexander is good and the Ender Dragon is evil. How could they . . . how—" I couldn't finish out loud, but my brain was going into overdrive. How could Steve Alexander and the Ender Dragon have worked together? Who was really good, and who was really evil?

The Ender Dragon had said, again and again, there was much I didn't know about Steve Alexander. She kept telling me to join her.

Was her side actually the side of good? Is that what the drawing meant?

No, no. Her side wanted to destroy the Overworld!

So if Steve Alexander had once worked with her, did that mean . . . he was evil too? Had this whole treacherous journey to find the Ender crystal shards meant nothing? Had everything Steve Alexander had written been a lie?

I sank to my knees. I had never felt so betrayed in my life. Because if Steve Alexander was evil, then all the legends about him were lies. All the statues were meaningless. Was the sky made of ground and the ground made of sky? If I couldn't believe this, what could I believe anymore?

"I'm with Stevie!" Alex said, wiping her hand over the page frantically as if to blot it out. "This can't be right!"

Maison and Destiny stared, openmouthed, at the page, as though transfixed. Yancy looked grim, as if he didn't like what he saw, but he accepted it. As if he'd accepted a lot of disappointment in his life and was more used to it than the rest of us. He'd lived a few years longer than us—as life went on, did you learn more and more terrible things about it?

"If it's in the book, it must be real," Yancy said quietly.

"There has to be an explanation for it," Maison said. She turned to the next page and ran the crystal across it frantically, trying to unlock something, anything.

"I get it now," I said miserably, pulling myself back up to my feet. "Remember how we couldn't figure out if the jungle temple we went to had belonged to Steve Alexander or the Ender Dragon? That's because it belonged to both of them. That's why we saw the claw marks and the S-A symbols for Steve Alexander. That's why we saw a picture of a dragon on the sign out front."

"That doesn't explain why there was a cell for Steve Alexander in the dungeon," Destiny pointed out.

My heart flip-flopped. She was right—that part still didn't make sense, and I wanted to believe in Steve Alexander. But now a terrible thought came into my head: How could I believe in someone I'd never even met?

You did *meet him,* I told himself. Well, not exactly. I'd heard his voice a few times. Still, it had been a good, helpful voice.

Just then I heard the voice again, as though I'd willed it into being. *I know what you must be thinking,* Steve Alexander's voice said.

Alex's head popped up. "Who's talking?"

"You mean you can hear him too?" I exclaimed. In the past, only I'd been able to hear Steve Alexander's voice, in my head. But everyone seemed to be alert and looking around.

This is my greatest shame, Steve Alexander's voice went on.

"His voice is coming from the book!" Maison cried. "The crystal must have triggered it."

If enough years have passed, maybe people have forgotten how I unleashed the Ender Dragon, his voice continued. *However, I will never forget. If you have retrieved this many shards of the crystal, you must be truly good, honest people, and hard workers. I asked my companion Maya to hide the crystals well, and I helped her enchant this book so that you would truly be able to see what happened, both before and after the battle.*

"See what happened?" Yancy repeated, quirking an eyebrow. "What does he mean by that?"

Until now, you have read my words, the voice said. *Now you will see my life.*

At that, we were all blinded by a bright light.

CHAPTER 4

HEN THE LIGHT FADED, WE WERE OUT-doors in the Overworld. There was no sign of Maison's bedroom, but the five of us (plus Blue) were all still together, and Maison was still holding the book.

"What happened?" Alex exclaimed, looking around. We were near a village, though it wasn't a village I recognized. People were milling about, and I saw there was a sign nearby that said, in giant letters, MONSTER-FIGHTING CONTEST TODAY.

"Excuse me!" Alex called to a man walking past her. The man ignored her, as if she wasn't even there. "How rude!" Alex huffed.

I watched the people walk by. You'd have thought they'd notice five kids showing up out of nowhere in a burst of light, especially when three of those kids were from Earth, and looked different from blocky

Overworld kids. Even so, no one even turned their head.

"I don't think they can see us," Maison said.

Yancy walked up to a passing man and poked him in the arm. The man kept walking without missing a beat.

"I'd say you're right," Yancy said. "Sooo . . . is this magical or creepy?"

"Why would Steve Alexander bring us here?" Alex asked.

"The real question is, how do we get back?" Destiny said, looking from side to side uneasily.

"Maybe the book will bring us back after we see what we're supposed to see," I said. I was pretty uneasy, myself. This didn't feel right at all. We were like ghosts here, and we didn't even know where "here" was! If I could have asked someone for a map, I might have felt a little less uncomfortable—at least then I'd have been able to find my way back home if necessary.

People were lining up by the MONSTER-FIGHTING CONTEST TODAY sign. Two men had large wooden swords, and they were swinging them around, looking proud of themselves. The swords looked like regular wooden swords, but bigger.

"We're going to win this contest, Drake," said one of the men to the other.

The other man laughed. "I know it, Mick!" he said.

"No one ever thought of making wooden swords . . . BIGGER!" hooted the one called Drake.

"Nuh-uh!" said Mick loudly. "We're geniuses."

Yancy sighed and put his hand over his eyes. "I guess you find that type in every world."

"Uh-oh, Drake. Look who's coming," said Mick.

"Is it our lil friend?" asked Drake. You could tell, from the mocking way he said it, that he didn't really consider this person his friend.

Another man was stepping up to join them beside the sign, looking uncertain. A white dog with a red collar walked next to him.

My mouth fell open. The man's posture was unfamiliar—like someone trying to sneak by unnoticed—but his features were unmistakable. His square beard, his dark hair. No wonder people said Dad and I looked like him. He was even carrying a diamond sword.

"It's our lil Steve Alexander," Mick said with a smirk.

CHAPTER 5

"OH, UH, HI, GUYS," STEVE ALEXANDER STAM-mered. I couldn't believe it. Steve Alexander stammering!

He tried to make his way past Mick and Drake, only to have Drake grab him by the sleeve. The dog let out a low growl.

"What do you think you're doing, showing your face here again?" Drake asked. "You should have learned your lesson last year."

"He should have learned his lesson when we were kids," Mick cut in, and the two of them laughed.

"I really should be going," Steve Alexander said, and tried to free himself from Drake's grip. Drake just dug in harder.

"Hold on," Drake said. "We've known each other since we were little. Don't you want to catch up with us?"

"Not really," Steve Alexander said.

"That's so cold!" Mick said. "Why not?"

Steve Alexander looked back and forth between them. "Well, when we were kids, you used to steal my inventions and hide them . . ."

"Oh, yeah!" Mick said, chuckling again. "That was funny!"

"Hey, remember the first time we tried to make him ride a horse?" Drake said. "He fell off, so we took the horse's lead and strung him up with it. He was just dangling there upside down by his ankle."

"That was great!" Mick said. "He looked like a toy!"

Leads were strips used to tame and ride horses in the Overworld, but I'd never heard of them being used to tie someone up like that. These guys were cruel!

"That wasn't great," Steve Alexander said. "I could have gotten really hurt. Now, if you'll excuse me . . ."

"Wait a second," Mick said. He got serious and stepped in close, eyeing the diamond sword Steve Alexander carried. "What's this thing you got?"

"That's, uh, my invention," Steve Alexander said. "It's a sword made of diamonds."

Drake and Mick looked at each other for a second. They tried to keep straight faces, but they clearly couldn't. They both burst out laughing, and Drake had to let go of Steve Alexander's shirt to bend over and clutch his sides when he laughed too hard. Mick was slapping his knee at the hilarity.

"A sword made out of diamonds!" Mick roared. "That's the dumbest thing—"

"There's no way you're going to beat us!" Drake said. "We made wooden swords!"

"Wooden swords already exist," Steve Alexander said.

"Yeah, but these are BIGGER!" Drake said.

"So much BIGGER!" Mick said.

Steve Alexander turned to walk away, his dog following.

"Hey, wait up!" Drake said as he and Mick chased after him. "You aren't still sore about *last* year's monster-fighting contest, are you?"

"When you won the contest because you made slightly bigger wooden swords, and I lost even though I discovered the Nether?" Steve Alexander muttered. "No, not at all."

"We took something useful and made it bigger," Mick said. "And bigger always means better."

"Whereas you made that weird portal," Drake said. "It looked all great at first, until people started going in there and getting attacked by ghasts and zombie pig-men. What were you thinking?"

"I was thinking the Nether had a lot to offer—" Steve Alexander began.

"Well, you failed," Mick said. "And we won!"

"Don't forget *that* invention," Drake said, pointing at Steve Alexander's four-legged companion. "What do you call that, again?"

"A dog," Steve Alexander said.

"A dog!" Mick said. "Who in their right mind would want a dog?"

"He's a guard and a—" Steve Alexander began, only to be cut off.

"Remember when you showed everyone your dog?" Drake said. "What happened? A bunch of people tried to tame wolves. And they just got bitten."

"They didn't know what they were doing, but—" Steve Alexander tried to get in.

"They got hurt because of you!" Mick said.

"Gentlemen, is something the matter here?" interrupted a woman who was hurrying over with a confident stride. She had red hair and a serious expression.

"Mayor Pandra!" Steve Alexander cried, looking awed by her. "I'm sorry, miss, I'm just trying to get my stuff ready for the contest . . ."

With that red hair of hers, Mayor Pandra looked a lot like Aunt Alexandra and Alex. I glanced at Alex and could tell from her wide, riveted eyes that she was already enthralled with this woman.

Mayor Pandra edged over toward Mick and Drake. "You understand we hold this contest every year because of our monster problem," she said. "We are here to work together to fight *monsters*, not to tear one another down. This contest is about celebrating the best minds in the Overworld."

"Then why'd you let Steve Alexander in?" Drake said. Mick snickered behind his hand.

Mayor Pandra's mouth curled downward in disgust. "Steve Alexander is welcome here, just as everyone else is," she said. "I expect you two to treat him better."

She looked down at the dog. "He doesn't bite, does he?"

"Oh, no, no, no," Steve Alexander said quickly, almost tripping over his own words. "I named him Wolf, but he was only a wolf until I tamed him. Now he's a dog, but I've named him Wolf . . ."

Drake and Mick were laughing in the background, unable to help themselves. Steve Alexander did sound pretty silly right then, as if he couldn't get the right words out, no matter how hard he tried.

It looked like the mayor wanted to say more, but another villager was calling her over. "If you'll excuse me, gentlemen," she said, walking away breezily.

Steve Alexander watched her go, looking somehow awestruck, grateful, and embarrassed that he'd needed someone else to stick up for him.

"She's right, Mick," Drake said. "I think we've been too hard on Steve Alexander."

"Yeah, Drake," Mick said. "We should give him a present."

"A present?" Steve Alexander said timidly, as if he didn't know what to expect.

When they brought him his present a minute later, his eyes widened in horror.

"What?" Mick said. "It's just a horse. You like horsies, don't you, Steve Alexander?"

"You're not still scared of horses, are you?" teased Drake. "You? Big, brave Steve Alexander, who discovered the Nether and tamed a wolf?"

"I'm . . ." Steve Alexander started. He stopped, swallowed, and tried again. "I'm not scared of horses."

"Then ride it," Drake said.

"Hey, everyone!" Mick shouted to the crowds. "Look at Steve Alexander's great horse-riding skills!"

Everyone in the area turned to look. I glanced around for Mayor Pandra, though she was long gone.

"What, you don't like our gift?" Drake said, watching Steve Alexander's panicky face. "You should be grateful!"

The people began chanting for Steve Alexander to get on the horse. A number of them were laughing. What was going on here?

Steve Alexander looked around nervously, but it seemed he couldn't find any way out of this. Slowly, he crept up to the horse, looking at it as if it were a monster about to attack. The horse just stood there patiently. Why was Steve Alexander so scared of it? It looked just like a regular horse. Was he still scared because of what happened so many years ago?

But when he tried climbing on the animal's back, the horse wouldn't have it. It threw back its head, whinnying, and knocked Steve Alexander to the ground. He landed on the seat of his pants, letting out a groan. The whole crowd burst out laughing.

"This never gets old!" Drake whooped, holding his stomach with laughter.

Guffaws roared all around us. His face twisted in pain, Steve Alexander jumped to his feet and fled.

CHAPTER 6

THE WHITE LIGHT SHOWED UP AGAIN, SWEEPING us along with Steve Alexander so we wouldn't lose track of him. It was almost like watching a movie in Maison's world. Except all of this was real. These were actual scenes from the past!

We'd been so caught up in what we were watching that no one had spoken for a while. Now Destiny said as we moved in the wave of light, "I feel so bad for Steve Alexander."

"Yeah," Maison said. "It took me a while to get the hang of taming and riding horses in *Minecraft*. I can see how it would be hard for him."

"It's not only that," Yancy said. "He does all these smart things and no one sees it. Then there's one simple thing he can't do, and the others rub it in."

"But what sort of hero can't ride a horse?" Alex said, looking offended at the very idea.

The sort of hero in front of us, apparently. After running past the village, Steve Alexander reached the edge of a jungle biome, where he stopped to catch his breath. The light vanished and we were just standing at the scene. Steve Alexander hit one of the jungle trees in frustration, slashing clear through it with his sword. "Stupid, stupid," he said, hitting himself in the head with his free hand. Then something caught his attention.

It was a dark mineshaft, leading down below the ground.

The dog called Wolf had followed Steve Alexander to the edge of the jungle. He looked at the mineshaft and whined.

Despite this, Steve Alexander started going down into the mineshaft, striking out with his sword and hitting the block walls to find his way in the dark. Wolf followed him like a shadow, watching with worried eyes. And we followed both of them like ghosts. Soon Steve Alexander's sword hit nothing but air, and he seemed to realize he'd found an opening to another room. When he stepped inside, his jaw dropped in amazement.

The room's walls were lined with stone bricks, and in the center of the room was an enormous portal, hovering over an open pool of bright-red lava and connected to the ground by a small set of stairs. It was an End portal! I knew that End portals were super rare, and I guessed from Steve Alexander's expression that he'd never seen one before this. He hesitantly walked up the steps, one eye on the lava below so he wouldn't accidentally fall.

The portal was framed with a dozen blocks that had green eyes in them, and the middle looked like a starry sky. He touched the edge of the portal with his hand, then jumped back with a startled bellow. An Enderman was coming out of the portal! I expected an attack, but Steve Alexander quickly ducked away, and the Enderman ignored him. Usually Endermen only attacked you if you looked them in the eye. This Enderman was carrying a small purple crystal in its hands. An Ender crystal! Then the mob teleported and Steve Alexander and Wolf were alone again.

"So, is this where the Endermen come from?" Steve Alexander murmured to himself, rising to check out the portal again. "If so, I'll call it the End. Maybe I can go exploring there later. I might discover new . . ." Then he stopped speaking, and his face clouded over.

"Nothing I do matters," he said, angry once more. "I could save this whole world and they wouldn't accept me! Not even her . . . not even Mayor Pandra . . ." He trailed off sadly, until anger overtook him again. "It's always Mick and Drake, everywhere I turn! They've tormented me for years. If only they knew what it felt like to suffer, then maybe they would understand!"

He slammed his diamond sword so hard into the wall that it stuck in the stone. He stood there, panting and sweaty, staring at the sword, then looked ashamed at himself. "What am I saying?" he whispered, so low I could barely hear it.

Suddenly, a faint voice called out, as though far off in the darkness of the mineshaft. "I know what it's like to suffer."

Steve Alexander jerked back. "Who's there?" With a lurch, he pulled his diamond sword out of the wall. And he drew a torch from his toolkit so he could see better.

"Please," the voice called. It sounded raspy and powerless, like whoever was speaking was too weak to come to him. Steve Alexander walked farther and farther down the mineshaft, toward the voice, with us following close behind. Minutes passed, and it felt as if he must be in the deepest depths of the mineshaft by now. "Please, please release me," the voice continued to call.

And when Steve Alexander turned the next corner, he discovered a dragon.

CHAPTER 7

THE ENDER DRAGON! ONLY . . . SHE DIDN'T LOOK the way she had when I'd seen her in the End, a creature full of power and might flying over everyone's heads. She didn't look evil, or sound it. She was crouching low to the ground, as if she were hurt, her large body confined to the tight walls of the mineshaft. Her black form almost seemed part of the darkness, but her purple eyes glowed brightly in the torchlight.

When Steve Alexander entered the room she was in, she tried to sit up and lift her tail. But there just wasn't enough space, and her head bumped into the ceiling. When she moved, I saw her legs were chained.

And there were purple crystals linked in the chains. More Ender crystals!

"I've heard of dragons in stories," Steve Alexander said, shocked, "but I never knew them to be real!"

"Yes," she said, looking down at him. "I have been trapped here so, so long."

Wolf stepped up behind his master, took one look at the dragon, and started to growl.

"Wolf, no!" Steve Alexander scolded. He turned back to the dragon and asked gently, "Who did this to you?"

"People who did not understand me," she said. "They saw I was different and judged me."

Steve Alexander looked sympathetic. "How long have you been chained down here?"

"For centuries, I think," she said.

"You poor thing," he said, stepping closer and laying a gentle hand on her flank. She heaved a sad sigh, the force of her breath almost lifting him off his feet. If I hadn't seen it for my own eyes, I never could have imagined the Ender Dragon was capable of looking so vulnerable and mistreated. Right then, even I felt sorry for her.

"Let me get you out of these chains," he said.

"Your sword will not break these," she said. "No sword can."

"But I have a new sword," Steve Alexander said. He took his diamond sword to one of her shackles. With just one blow, the sword shattered the chain.

The Ender Dragon's eyes glowed even brighter. "Such power!" she said.

Steve Alexander grinned a little sheepishly as he freed her next leg. "It's my newest invention," he said. "A diamond sword."

"A diamond sword!" she marveled. "Do you have other inventions?"

"Well, I created a portal to a new world I call the Nether, and right now I'm experimenting with redstone," he said. "Speaking of the Nether, I found a strange thing in the mineshaft here that looks like a portal, and an Enderman came out of it. Do you have any idea what it is?"

"It's nothing," she said. "An old relic from times long past. Tell me more about your redstone work, and the weapons you've created. What do you use them for?"

Steve Alexander clearly enjoyed her interest and attention. "I think I can use the redstone to make things move on their own," he said. "And so far the diamond sword is the strongest sword I've been able to invent."

"Surely, you must be loved by your people for these great creations," she said. "Have they made you a king for such greatness?"

"A king?" He looked up at her, surprised, then cut through the last of the chains. "I don't know about *that*." He stood and surveyed his work. "There you go. You're free!"

"How can I ever repay you for this?" she asked, swinging her tail.

"Oh, don't mention it." I thought I saw a blush creep up his face, like he was embarrassed to say what he really wanted.

Still, the Ender Dragon guessed that he had an idea. "There must be something."

"Well." He looked up at her looming form. Steve Alexander and the dragon were two different sizes and two different species, but right then they were the same—two total outsiders. "If you're misunderstood and I'm misunderstood, maybe we can be misunderstood together. Will you be my friend?"

"A friend?" she repeated. "Ah, this world has changed from the one I knew. Friendship has never been offered to me before now."

"Then let's be friends, you and I," he said. "I have a home some distance from here, but I've always wanted to build a new one in the jungle, where I can be away from people. We can build a home big enough for both of us, right near here."

"What luck that we have found each other," she agreed.

"Come on," he said, sounding eager now. "I'll lead you to the surface. If we have each other, we won't need anyone else."

He quickly led her through the mineshaft, bouncing with each step. Wolf trotted along at his side, ever faithful. The Ender Dragon followed more slowly behind, her large body filling the mineshaft as she swayed through it. They passed the End portal room, and Steve Alexander didn't ask about it again.

"It will be nice to see sunlight after so many years in darkness," the Ender Dragon said fondly.

But when they rose to the surface, it was overcast. Rain sprinkled on the Ender Dragon's snout. As she emerged from the darkness of the mineshaft, I could see just how enormous she really was. She stood tall as a building behind Steve Alexander.

"Sorry about the weather," Steve Alexander said. "It should clear up soon."

Then a scream echoed from the distance, and he tensed, turning. "The village!" he cried. "The overcast sky is letting mobs out! They must be attacking the village!"

"Show me where you want to build our home in the jungle biome," the Ender Dragon said, turning toward the trees and vines near them.

"But what about the villagers?" Steve Alexander cried. "What about the mayor?"

She looked back over her enormous shoulder at him. "I thought you didn't care about them. Or do you just care about the mayor?"

"I—I—" Steve Alexander stammered. He caught himself and said, "Even if I don't like them, I can't just leave them in danger!" Just then, I could see an idea struck him. It crossed his face like a light turning on.

"Dragon!" he called up to her. "Will you help me protect the villagers?"

CHAPTER 8

THE NEXT THING I KNEW, WE WERE BACK IN THE village. Steve Alexander's guess had been right—with the overcast sky, the village was overrun by zombies! The zombies had torn down the contest sign and were chasing people into their houses. People weren't even safe in their homes, because the zombies easily tore through their wooden doors. I saw Mayor Pandra was fighting off a zombie with a wooden sword, but wooden swords were about as useful as wooden doors. And after all that bragging about their new, bigger wooden swords, I saw Mick and Drake hiding under a table and clinging to each other. Zombies surrounded them, closing in.

"Hit them, Drake!" Mick yelled.

"No, you hit them, Mick!" Drake yelled back.

They wimpily shook their wooden swords at the zombies. One zombie ripped the sword out of Mick's hand and broke it in two in the process.

"That's not fair!" Mick said. "We made the swords bigger!"

They huddled closer together, not even trying to protect themselves anymore.

Then a black shape appeared in the sky. As the shadow drew closer, the features of the Ender Dragon became visible. Her wings were flapping furiously, and Steve Alexander was riding on her back, sword held up high.

As they came into the village, the Ender Dragon opened her mouth and spewed purple-colored fireballs all over the zombies, freezing them in their tracks. This gave the people the opportunity to run at the mobs with their wooden swords. The zombies around Drake and Mick froze, and villagers rushed over to take care of them. I noticed Drake and Mick didn't come out from their hiding spot. But they both lifted their heads and looked around them with am-I-really-seeing-this expressions.

The Ender Dragon swung down low to the ground, her wings almost brushing the houses, blasting more purple fireballs from her mouth while Steve Alexander reached down and struck zombies with his diamond sword. One hit from that sword was enough to make a zombie disappear.

The tide of the battle was turning before our eyes.

When the Ender Dragon reached the edge of the village, she swept back around to fly over it again. The Ender Dragon's breath and Steve Alexander's sword quickly finished off any zombies that remained from the first sweep. And as the last of the zombies vanished, the clouds parted in the sky and sunlight poured down on the scene. The Ender Dragon gracefully landed in the grass, folding her wings.

Steve Alexander slid off her back, and when his feet hit the ground, everyone in the area started cheering, except for Mick and Drake.

At first Steve Alexander looked surprised by all the cheering. But as the applause went on, he seemed to realize it was for him. For him and the dragon. Meanwhile, Wolf came running safely into the village and joined his master, his tongue lolling happily out of his mouth.

"Steve Alexander saved us!" I recognized the voice of Mayor Pandra. She came out of the crowd and stood before him. "Steve Alexander and the dragon!"

"It was nothing, really," Steve Alexander said. He looked sort of embarrassed, but I could also tell he was really enjoying himself.

"Hey, he just got lucky!" Mick said, pulling himself out from under a table. He was still holding his broken wooden sword. "A few more seconds, and we would have had those zombies!" Just then, another piece of his sword broke off and fell to the ground.

"Yeah!" said Drake hotly. "Don't forget: Steve Alexander can't even ride a horse. He's not special."

"Who cares if he can't ride a horse?" a villager jeered at Drake. "He can ride a *dragon*!"

Steve Alexander's chest puffed out with the praise. "I wouldn't have been able to do this without my new friend," he said, turning to the Ender Dragon. "My diamond sword could have only done so much."

"We must honor both of you for your great courage," Mayor Pandra said. She handed Steve Alexander a medal she'd pulled out of her cloak. "And it goes without saying that you won this year's contest."

He took the medal, beaming.

"What is your name, dragon?" Mayor Pandra asked, looking up at her. "So that we can always honor it in our village."

The Ender Dragon tilted her head as if she'd never heard this question. "My name?"

"You don't have a name?" Steve Alexander looked up at her in disbelief. "Everyone needs to have a name. Even Wolf has a name!"

Wolf gave a happy bark.

"You named your tamed wolf . . . Wolf?" the Ender Dragon said. "Then are you going to name me Dragon?"

He shook his head. "The name Dragon might scare people off, but everyone should know your kindness." He thought about it for a moment. "I know!" he said, beaming up at her. "We'll name you Jean!"

CHAPTER 9

I T HIT ME LIKE A TON OF BRICKS. "JEAN!" I CRIED. I'D been so caught up in what I was watching I could barely think about our mission to find the Ender crystal shards. But now my mind was flashing back to the haunted jungle temple, where we'd found notes inviting people to a party put on by Steve Alexander and J—. And that was it. All the papers had been so old that we hadn't been able to find a single card with the full name of the second person. No, not person—the full name of the *dragon*.

I looked at Maison, Alex, Destiny, and Yancy, and saw they'd already come to the same conclusion.

"This is . . . a lot more complicated than I expected," Destiny said.

"Life is complicated," Yancy said. "And . . . I guess sometimes even life inside video games is complicated."

The white light was coming up around us again.

We were about to see something different! The next thing I knew, the five of us were deep in the jungle, surrounded by trees and vines. Parrots chirped in the branches. From his perch on Yancy's shoulder, Blue chirped back.

Steve Alexander was working on constructing a massive building in front of us, Wolf at his side. The Ender Dragon—or should I call her Jean?—was helping him carry supplies for what he was making.

"It's the jungle temple!" I exclaimed, my heart *thump-thump*ing. "They're making it together!"

What was going on here? This dragon was helpful, and I knew there was no way the evil Ender Dragon would help save a village! Maybe this wasn't the Ender Dragon. Were there two dragons? Were they twins? My head hurt trying to figure all this out.

"Hey, someone's coming," Maison said.

We all turned toward the sound of people making their way through the jungle. Wolf came over to investigate, walking right past us as if we weren't there, even though the dog came so close his fur brushed against my sleeve.

I saw Mayor Pandra and a few other people were inching through all the trees, trying not to stumble. Steve Alexander looked up, did a double-take, and then ran over.

"Mayor Pandra!" he exclaimed. "Do you need any help?"

She stumbled on a vine and he caught her before

she fell. Then, looking embarrassed, he quickly let her go.

"Thank you," she said. "We were hoping we could talk to you and Jean . . ." She trailed off and stared in awe at the partly-made jungle temple. "What is this?"

"It's a special home for Jean and me!" Steve Alexander said eagerly. "Come, I'll show you."

He walked her through parts of the building, pointing out the trapdoors and hidden passageways.

"So fancy!" she said. "But it seems dangerous for guests."

"It's just to keep us safe, way out in the jungle here," he said. "Look, I want to show you the redstone I've been working with. Watch this." He pressed a switch and a minecart zigzagged through the hall. The mayor clapped her hands over her mouth in astonishment.

"You can make it move without touching it!" she marveled.

"Yeah," he said. "Some villages have asked to use the invention, so I'm starting to get a little bit of a name for myself."

She put her hands back down. "That really does seal it, then. Steve Alexander, I came to ask you a favor."

"A favor?" he repeated. Jean was following along behind, watching them talk. "What?"

"I want you and Jean to help the people of the Overworld fight mobs," she said. "What you did in the village a few weeks ago was incredible. With all your inventions, and with your ability to ride a dragon,

I think we could be seeing a bright new day for our world."

"I don't know how much I can do . . ." he started to say.

She grabbed his arm. "Yes, you do!" she insisted. "All the people in our village are already mining diamonds to make diamond swords. They saw how much better your sword was than their wooden swords. And you said yourself that some villages are interested in your redstone work. We need to spread this knowledge more. And each night, if you can ride your dragon and chase away the mobs harassing villagers . . . oh, how amazing that would be!"

It looked like he didn't want to tell her no, but he was hesitant. He turned to the dragon. "What do you think, Jean? This would involve you too."

"I trust you to know what is best for us," Jean said calmly. I kept watching her, waiting for some clue that she was going to turn evil, or some proof she was a dragon different from the Ender Dragon I knew. "I await your decision."

Mayor Pandra looked back at him with begging eyes.

Slowly, Steve Alexander said, "If it's fine with Jean, it's fine with me."

"Wonderful!" Mayor Pandra cheered. "There's something I want to show you."

She pulled out a piece of paper with a sketch on it. The sketch showed a heroic-looking Steve Alexander riding Jean, her long black wings spread wide as she flew.

"I want to make a statue of this in our village," she said. "It's just a design now, so first I wanted to see what you thought of it."

"It's . . . it's incredible," Steve Alexander said, as if he could barely believe it. Jean hung her heavy head over Steve's shoulder to get a good look, too.

"It wouldn't surprise me if before long there's a statue like this in every village of the Overworld," the mayor went on.

I could tell her words were really getting Steve Alexander pumped up. He handed the paper back to her and said to Jean, "It'll be dark within an hour. What do you say we start flying to villages now, to make sure they're safe?"

In response, Jean lowered herself to the ground so he could climb on her back. As soon as he was comfortably settled, she ambled out of the temple and took off for the sky.

"The Overworld will never be the same!" Mayor Pandra called up to them as they flew away.

And then the white light came in again, pulling us into another scene.

CHAPTER 10

"I DON'T KNOW WHAT TO THINK," I ADMITTED, AS we watched scene after scene showing Steve Alexander and Jean saving villages from mob attacks. Their battles all looked like the first one, with Jean sweeping down and shooting her fiery purple breath and Steve Alexander taking out mobs left and right with his sword.

"This is clearly a different dragon," Alex said with an eye roll. "Just because they look the same doesn't mean they are the same."

"I don't know," Yancy said, his hand to his chin. "People can change. Why not dragons, too?"

"I think we just need to watch and learn," Maison said. "My mom always said you can't jump to conclusions. You have to learn all about something before you have an opinion on it."

Yancy snorted. "Not in the days of the Internet.

The more knee-jerk your reaction online, the more the Internet seems to reward you for it."

"Guys, shh," Destiny said. "The scene is changing."

After the village rescues, we saw different villages putting up statues of Steve Alexander and the Ender Dragon. At one point we watched Steve Alexander and Jean proudly posing for an artist who was making an enormous, blocky statue. We also saw a lot of cheering crowds, and villagers and mayors handing them medals. If Steve Alexander had once been a loser, he was now the most popular person in the Overworld.

We also saw how his life was changing. After making his large jungle temple, he built a whole lot of other mansions around the Overworld. He was sure on the up and up. There was a scene where he and Mayor Pandra got married, and a few scenes later we saw him, the mayor, and a little boy running around. I guessed that must have been their son, Steve. I wasn't sure how many years were passing with each new scene now. But in each group scene we saw more people with diamond swords. We could see redstone being used in some backgrounds. Steve Alexander's inventions were definitely making their way around the world—and people were loving them.

Well, apparently not everyone.

"I hate him!" Mick said in one scene. He was standing with Drake at the back of a crowd, watching Steve Alexander accept another village medal.

"I know!" Drake said. "I asked him, 'Are you going

to make your diamond swords bigger?' He said, 'No, I'm going to try enchanting swords to make them more powerful.' What a snob!"

"No kidding!" Mick said. "He only thinks about himself."

"He has the whole Overworld eating out of his hand," Drake said. "He wouldn't be so fancy if he didn't have that dragon friend."

Mick's face lit up. "Hey, I have an idea! Let's steal his dragon!"

"You numbskull!" Drake said. "How are we going to steal a dragon?"

"We could make bigger wooden swords," Mick offered. Drake grabbed him by the shirt and shook him.

"No sword is ever going to be big enough to steal a dragon!" Drake said.

"Excuse me," said a person in the crowd. "I couldn't help overhearing what you were saying about Steve Alexander. Do you know him?"

"Known him since childhood!" Drake bragged, letting go of Mick. "Why?"

"I'd be interested in hearing your stories," said the person. He gave them a greasy smile.

In the next scene, Steve Alexander was home at night in the jungle temple, reading a book to Steve. The Ender Dragon was lying behind him, watching them, her long wings stretched out. Mayor Pandra walked over timidly, as if she had something bad she wanted to say.

"Steve?" she said to the boy. "Why don't you go play for a few minutes?"

"Can I play with Jean?" the boy asked eagerly.

"That's fine," Jean said, and she got up and lumbered out of the room with Steve. As soon as they were gone, Steve Alexander asked, "What's wrong?"

"When I was in the village today, people were saying horrible things about you," Mayor Pandra said. "Apparently Mick and Drake have been spreading all sorts of mean, nasty stories, and people are believing them."

Steve Alexander shrugged. "I can't control what people believe. Besides, Mick and Drake have always had it in for me."

"The other people don't know that. They just know Mick and Drake were childhood friends of yours—"

Steve Alexander made a face. "Mick and Drake were never my friends."

"Well, they're people who have known you, so other people trust what they have to say."

"Those guys never even knew me well," he replied.

"They say you're not very smart, the only reason you're famous is because you have a dragon, and that you only think about yourself."

"I go out every night with Jean to fight mobs," he protested, clearly hurt. "That doesn't sound like someone who only thinks of himself! Mick and Drake just like to tear down anyone who is different, especially if someone is successful through their own hard work."

"I'm sure it will pass over soon," she said.

Apparently, it didn't. The next scene we saw was another annual monster fighting contest, and Steve Alexander showed up with his newly enchanted diamond sword. Anyone could tell from the look on his face that he expected to win. For the first time, I saw that full-of-himself expression.

He and Jean were shocked when the votes were tallied and the people had decided that Drake and Mick's new invention—a bigger minecart—was the star of the show.

"You see, your invention isn't really new," one of the contest judges explained afterward to a shocked Steve Alexander. "It's just the same old sword with a new enchantment."

"But how is that minecart any better?" Steve Alexander demanded.

"It can fit more things," the judge said. "That means people have to take fewer trips and carry less."

"This is ridiculous," Jean cut in. "That's a double standard. You can't say one object can't win because of an improvement, yet another can."

"Sorry," the judge said. "You're not from around here. You just don't get it."

Jean's lips curled back and I saw her fangs for the first time. I'd never seen those fangs, even during all their battles.

That's when Steve Alexander exploded.

"It's all because of them!" he yelled, pointing

savagely at Drake and Mick, who were holding their medals and smirking. "They turned you against me! You'd rather listen to their lies than see what I've done! Why?"

People were shocked by his outburst. I heard a woman say, "I don't want my kids looking up to him, if he acts this way." A man said, "You know, I went down to the Nether once after he discovered it. I threw a rock at a zombie pigman and a whole group of them attacked me. That never would have happened if it weren't for Steve Alexander."

Hearing these words, Steve Alexander whirled around. "You don't just throw rocks at zombie pig-men!" he shouted. "That's why they attacked you!"

"No!" the man shouted back. "I never would have known about the Nether at all if it weren't for you."

"I can't believe I'm hearing this," Steve Alexander said, wild-eyed. "You people should be thanking me! Why did you all turn against me?"

The crowd continued to complain. Jean said darkly, "Let's go." Her words echoed like thunder in the sky as the two of them turned and left.

CHAPTER 11

A T DINNER THAT NIGHT, STEVE ALEXANDER WAS still sulking. After he told his wife all about it, she said, "It shouldn't matter if you won the award or not. What matters is helping other people."

"You'd think they'd be more grateful," he said, stabbing at his beef. "A few years ago, everyone loved me and built statues of me. Now . . . this."

"People still love you," she said. "You shouldn't listen to the mean voices out there. There are always going to be mean voices, but most people are nicer than that."

"Hmph," Yancy said next to me.

I had been so absorbed in what I was watching that I startled and looked at him. "What?" I asked.

"It's just like Earth," Yancy said. "Some people choose to be nicer, and some people choose to be meaner. And when you're successful like Steve

Alexander, there are going to be some people who get jealous of your success and take it out on you."

"Do you think that's what's going on?" I asked. I'd been really shocked by so many people turning against Steve Alexander.

"Well, that's part of it," Yancy said. "His meltdown at the contest today was something, though. It's like he needs their praise constantly or he can't stand it."

"Yeah," Maison said. "Don't you think the reward of helping people should be enough for him?"

Maybe it should have been, but I could also understand why Steve Alexander liked all the applause, and why he'd been frustrated when he did so much for the Overworld only to have people complain about him. I thought the guy complaining about the Nether seemed especially silly. Steve Alexander had found the Nether, but it had been the man's own careless actions that made the zombie pigmen attack him. Maybe the man thought it would be easier to blame Steve Alexander than admit he'd made a mistake.

I thought about the times I'd gotten jealous of other kids because they seemed to have it better than me. Sometimes they had better things because they'd worked hard for them, and sometimes those things had just been given to them. Either way, I knew that feeling of jealousy, and it was never a good feeling.

This whole thing—Steve Alexander, Mick, and Drake—it seemed like all of them wanted to be the number one person out there, the person who always got praise and never messed up. And they didn't seem very happy trying to get to be number one.

I watched Steve Alexander give a big sigh and glance toward Jean, who had just returned to her corner of the room. There was a fireplace nearby and the flames were dancing shadows along her large body. The fire also seemed to glow in her purple eyes.

"What do you think, Jean?" Steve Alexander asked her.

She looked away from the fire. "I think this reminds me of a long time ago, when the people turned against me," she said. "I'd done nothing to deserve it, but being different was enough for people not to like me."

Steve Alexander thumped his fist on the table, making his plate jump. "Why are people so fickle?"

"I think I have an idea," Jean offered. Her voice was soft.

"What's that?" Steve Alexander asked.

"Let's have an enormous party at our home, here in the jungle," she said. "We'll invite everyone. There will be feasting and dancing and speeches. We'll remind people what we've done for them. Everyone will feel excited by the talks and the food, and they will go away remembering what a hero Steve Alexander is."

He seemed to consider this. "Do you think it will work?"

Maybe it was just the shadow of the flames, but her smile looked sinister. "I'll make it work."

"All right," he said. "As long as we don't invite Drake and Mick."

"Oh," she said, dipping her head down, "we must especially invite Drake and Mick."

CHAPTER 12

I N THE NEXT SCENE, IT WAS THE NIGHT OF THE party and the jungle temple looked incredible. When my friends and I had explored the temple searching for an Ender crystal shard, it had been dark and spooky and long-abandoned. Now, it was full of decorations and tables and happy, laughing people holding their invitations that read: *We cordially invite you to a feast in the temple jungle, where we celebrate the victories of Steve Alexander and Jean.*

My stomach somersaulted. This was it. When we'd been searching for this jungle temple, a man from a nearby jungle village had told us that something terrible had happened at this temple. And when we'd found the temple, there had been plenty of evidence of destruction to back his story up. This had to be when it all happened.

The party was mostly taking place in the main

room, the large room we'd explored while searching for the crystal shard—where we'd seen claw marks on the walls and the word HELP etched in the stone. Now the room was full of torches and happy people who were talking and eating at the long tables as we stood there, invisible.

At the front of the room, seated at the largest table, were Steve Alexander and Jean. It was a very large table, so it could fit both man and dragon comfortably. The dog Wolf was sitting at Steve Alexander's right, panting happily.

Steve Alexander had been sulking the last time we'd seen him, but with this big party going on, you could tell he was enjoying himself. Clearly, his mood went up and down depending on what the people were saying around him. I could understand. I felt a lot happier with my friends than I ever did around kids who were mean to me.

I noticed that Drake and Mick were seated up near Steve Alexander and Jean. Mick was gulping down so much water I thought he might choke. Drake was sticking big hunks of meat into his mouth, almost gagging. They were the only people in the room who didn't look happy. In fact, they looked miserable to be in a room where everyone was celebrating the guy they liked to pick on.

Who else was here? I saw Mayor Pandra at another table, wearing a nice dress. Her son Steve was with her, and he was wearing a shirt with a picture of a dragon on it. He sure loved dragons—but I guess that's what happens when you're basically raised by one!

Even with all the happy faces, I couldn't stop the sick feeling in my stomach, knowing something truly terrible was about to happen.

As people were finishing up their meals, someone began chanting for Steve Alexander to give a speech. The chanting spread to other people, until everyone in the room had joined in (except for Mick and Drake, of course).

Smiling, Steve Alexander stood up and gave a long speech on doing the right thing, being responsible, working hard and how much he loved to help the Overworld. All the words sounded good, but I didn't know how much his heart was in them. It almost sounded like he was just saying what he thought people expected him to say.

"I never would have been able to do any of this if it weren't for Jean," he said. "I call her my 'steed,' yet she is so much more than that. She is my friend. She is my helper. She is my fellow hero in the Overworld. It's time to listen to her speak."

Everyone applauded. Steve Alexander sat back down, and Jean slowly and elegantly stood.

"Thank you, Steve Alexander," she said. "The Overworld has changed in many ways since I was released from my prison."

She continued, nodding toward the nearby window, through which we could see the moon. "These days, people in the Overworld feel safe leaving their homes at night. When the party started earlier, it was daylight. Now it is dark, and yet we all feel safe.

"I see diamond swords everywhere I go, and I see people benefitting from the mob raids Steve Alexander and I have been doing for years now," she went on. "What a world we have created."

She lowered her head as if she were being shy. Everyone except for Drake and Mick applauded. But when Jean lifted her head back up, there was a glint in her eye and I could see her fangs.

"However, tonight is when the real creation begins," she said in a powerful voice, raising her head high. "Tonight, I will make the Overworld into the world it should always have been."

Steve Alexander looked up at her, confused. "Jean?" he said, unsure. "What are you talking about?"

"This," she said. Her tail slammed against the wall behind her three times. A signal. All the secret doors to the large room burst open, revealing an army of armed skeleton guards in the hidden space behind the room, their swords drawn and ready for battle. People jumped up from their chairs, screaming. They tried to run out of the room, only to find every entrance blocked by more skeletons with sharp, gleaming swords.

"For years I have worked for your world, and what thanks do I get?" Jean demanded loudly.

"Jean!" Steve Alexander cried, jumping up himself. "What are you doing?"

"What must be done," she said. "This entire building is surrounded by mobs who work for me now. You will find there is no escape."

"This is madness!" Mayor Pandra cried. "Jean, this isn't you!"

Jean said, "Arrest her first." Just like that, two skeletons were on the mayor. She tried to free herself but wasn't strong enough.

Seeing the first arrest, the skeletons marched farther into the room, shackling everyone they came into contact with. The room was full of screams.

Jean smiled hungrily. "The Overworld belongs to me now."

CHAPTER 13

"JEAN!" STEVE ALEXANDER WAILED. THE DRAGON swung her head around to look at him. Her purple eyes were lit up with flames, even though there was no fire nearby.

"I did it!" she cheered, her voice raspy. "Steve Alexander, you and I will no longer be disrespected in this world! We will finally be the rulers we deserve to be!"

"You can't do this!" he exclaimed. "Release my wife! Release everyone!"

"Why?" Jean snapped. "She never understood you. Only I understand you." To the skeleton guards, she shouted, "Take everyone to the dungeon! I will decide what to do with them later." Her eyes slanted down to where Mick and Drake were trying to hide under their table. "Except these two. Leave them here for my amusement."

Mick and Drake let out loud whimpers.

"Stop!" Steve Alexander shouted at the skeleton guards. When they didn't listen, he tried running in the direction of his family. Another skeleton guard was putting shackles on his son Steve. But when Steve Alexander got too close, skeleton guards raised their swords and put them in an X-shape, blocking him from getting through. He whirled back around to Jean.

"Jean!" he yelled. "Why?"

"Why?" she repeated.

Wolf charged through the crowded room toward Jean, barking and growling. A skeleton guard grabbed him and held him in place.

"I'll tell you why," she said. "Because the people here are the same as the people who chained me. Because if we do not take power for ourselves, someone else will take it from us."

"These people aren't like the people who chained you!" Steve Alexander shouted. "These people are here to celebrate us!"

She lashed her tail toward Drake and Mick, who were still under a table. "Pull them out," she ordered her skeleton guards.

Hundreds of skeleton guards were in the middle of marching people out of the room. A few stopped pointing their swords at people and pulled Drake and Mick out.

"String them up," she said.

A skeleton guard threw a lead up to the ceiling and tied Drake and Mick to it by their ankles. They were hanging upside down, totally at Jean's mercy. She struck the lead with her tail, making them swing like toys.

"Stop this!" Steve Alexander hollered.

Jean looked at him, surprised. "You don't like this? You can help me torment them."

"No!" he said. "This is wrong!"

"Didn't you say when you found me that you wished they could suffer, so they'd understand?" she asked.

He tried to answer, choking on his words. "I didn't mean that!" he finally cried. "I said that out of anger!"

"Oh, but you said it," she said. "Will you join me, Steve Alexander? Together, we will make the Overworld in our image. Forget the statues—statues can be broken. Heroes can be forgotten. But those in power will always have control."

Before he could answer, she turned to the crowd and barked, "Bow to me!"

I couldn't believe it. Dozens of people, even with their shackles held by skeletons, instantly bowed their heads. They weren't even putting up a fight.

But I saw Steve Alexander didn't bow. He stood straight up to Jean, his hands clutched at his sides, and called out, "The people will never bow to a cruel master!"

"She's not cruel!" someone insisted. It was Drake! He was still hanging upside down, swinging from the lead. "She's just misunderstood!"

Steve Alexander stared at him, unable to believe what he was hearing. "How could you say that?"

"Desperate times call for desperate measures," Drake said. "I think she knows what she's doing. I'll work for her!"

Some of the other people chorused that they would too. Steve Alexander took a step back, his face paling. Then he cried, "Drake, you only agree to work for evil because it will protect you! You can't tell me that you agree with her, not after she's done this to you!"

"You're not seeing the big picture," Drake said.

"Cut him down," Jean said.

A skeleton released Drake from the lead. He fell to the floor in a tumble and pulled himself back up, dusting off his clothes.

"Arm him," she said.

A skeleton handed Drake a sword.

Steve Alexander gritted his teeth. "I see the big picture, Drake," he said. "Ever since I was a kid, I thought there was something special about you and Mick that I could never attain. Now I see that it was all fake—just a trick to make people like you. You're just cowards."

"I am disappointed in you, Steve Alexander," Jean said. "I was hoping you would see the truth in what I'm saying and be my right-hand man. It looks like Drake will have to take your place. Unless you're willing to change your mind?"

"Never!" Steve Alexander shouted. "I always do what's right!"

"Do you?" she said. "You only enjoyed fighting monsters when it gave you glory. Would you do it if there weren't people to cheer you on? Your wife was right—you shouldn't have been disappointed not to get the medal. It should have been enough just to serve. Admit it, you're not as high and mighty as you think you are. Why do you think people turned against you? If you do good deeds with a sense of arrogance, the people will see it."

It seemed like those words hit close to home. It took him a second before he replied, "What about you, Jean? How could you have helped me in so many battles when this is what you wanted? You agreed to be my friend!"

"Friend?" she scoffed. "This never had anything to do with friendship. I saw the smartest man in the Overworld willing to break me free, so I watched and I learned. I was with you for every new weapon, every invention—I understand how all of them work, so none of them can be used against me. Traveling to different villages to fight monsters, I learned the new layout of the Overworld, so I knew how to best stack my armies. I'm one step ahead of everyone."

A cloud passed over Steve Alexander's eyes. "You were never chained for being different, were you?" He barely whispered the words, as if he couldn't believe them.

"No," she said. "I tried to take over the Overworld once before, and failed. But this time, I've learned from my mistakes. Humans will never capture me again. And either you join me, or you join the others in the dungeon."

"I will never join you, Jean!" he shouted, finding his voice again. "You're a traitor!"

She laughed lightly. "There is one more thing you should know about me. My name was never Jean, and I don't care to be called that again. It is time to bring back my real name." She tossed back her head, her eyes nothing but purple flames. "I am the Ender Dragon."

I sucked in a deep breath. It was true, it was all true!

Jean, now the Ender Dragon, turned to the skeleton guards. "Take Steve Alexander to the dungeon with the rest," she ordered. "Place him in the special cell I had made just in case he was stubborn."

Skeletons seized Steve Alexander. He didn't even struggle. What was wrong with him? He looked so haunted, as though he could barely take in everything that he'd just learned. His best friend was really his greatest enemy. And he couldn't say he was blameless—not when he had been the one to let her out and help her obtain this power. Not when some of her words rang true, like his quest for glory over goodness.

The hundreds of people in the party were still being marched down into the basement. Except for Drake, who was given new armor and placed at the right hand of the Ender Dragon, working as her new guard and assistant. Mick pled his case too, and the next thing we knew he also had his own sword and armor.

In the dungeon, people were screaming and crying. Steve Alexander was stone-faced. But then he looked up and saw the cell at the far end of the dungeon. Its door hung open, and over the top of it, it said THIS CELL IS HOME TO THE PRISONER STEVE ALEXANDER.

I was breathing really hard, watching everything unfold. I remembered seeing that cell when we'd explored the jungle temple in our time, and now I knew why it existed. It really had been made by the Ender Dragon, specifically to humiliate Steve Alexander!

Right when Steve Alexander was seeing this, we heard a noise. Skeletons nearby them had gotten ahold of Wolf and were trying to push the dog. Wolf yelped, wanting to be free. Steve Alexander's eyes became alert, darting to the cell and then at the skeleton guards mistreating Wolf. He must have been remembering that his dog had been the first one to try to tell him about the Ender Dragon's evil.

That's when Steve Alexander seemed to snap.

He jerked loose of the skeleton guards, slamming them into his cell door. The skeletons holding Wolf let him go and went after Steve Alexander instead. He struck them, knocking them back. "Go, Wolf!" he called.

He made a break for the closest wall of the dungeon, his dog racing behind him. "Even Jean doesn't know all the secret passageways here!" He slammed his fist against the wall, opening up a hidden door. Both he and Wolf disappeared through the doorway, the hole in the wall closing up just as the skeleton guards were reaching it.

Drake and Mick came sweeping into the dungeon, their grins and posture showing how much they were enjoying their new power as the Ender Dragon's helpers. Stabbing his sword around like someone important, Drake called out grandly, "I'm here to see Steve Alexander in his cell."

"You'll never see it, then!" Mayor Pandra was shouting at him from another cell. Young Steve was in the cell with her. You could tell he was scared, but not hurt. "He escaped through a hidden door only he knew about!"

"Escaped?" Drake went white.

"And he'll be back to free us all," she threatened.

"Drake," Mick whispered. "You have to tell the Ender Dragon."

Drake went even whiter. "No, you tell her, Mick!"

"You're the one who wanted to work for her, Drake!" Mick said.

"So did you, Mick!" Drake said.

"Only because you did first!" Mick said.

The two of them crept guiltily up the stairs. The Ender Dragon was lounging in the now-empty party room. A few armed skeletons marched through. Someone had traced HELP into the wall as they were being dragged away.

"How does the grand Steve Alexander look, locked away in his little cell?" the Ender Dragon asked, ready to savor the answer.

Drake and Mick looked at the ground.

Impatient, she snapped, "Well? Answer me!"

"You see, he—" Drake began.

"There was a hidden door and—" Mick added.

"Are you saying . . . that he escaped?" she asked, her voice low.

They nodded.

The Ender Dragon's fury exploded with an enormous roar, and she slashed at the wall in her anger, leaving claw marks embedded deep in the rock. Mick and Drake cried out and clung to each other.

"You idiots!" she thundered. "He's the only one who might be able to stop me!" She turned to the skeleton guards. "Go—go out into the night and find him! Send every mob in the Overworld to look for him. He will not be able to hide for long!"

The skeleton guards spilled out of the temple into the darkness. I saw Steve Alexander in the distance with Wolf, running through the tangle of trees and vines. He could hear the hisses of zombies and the shrieks of armed skeletons on his tail. And over all the noises, he could still hear the roars of the Ender Dragon, erupting from the jungle temple as she howled for his capture.

CHAPTER 14

STEVE ALEXANDER AND WOLF DUCKED INTO A mineshaft—the same one in which they'd first found the Ender Dragon. Steve Alexander leaned back against the mineshaft's wall until he caught his breath. Then he began tearing through the mineshaft, as if looking for clues.

"How could I have been so blind?" he exclaimed. "Wolf, you were right all along!"

Wolf licked Steve Alexander's hand.

"She has my wife," he choked out. "She has my son. She helped *raise* my son. And now . . ."

He looked like he was close to losing it, just then. But I saw him push his sadness and fear down. He stood taller, his teeth clenched, determination on his face.

"I won't let her keep them!" he shouted. "I'll free everyone, and I'll stop her!"

Steve Alexander and Wolf went into the room where they'd first found the Ender Dragon, and I watched my ancestor start to dig in the ground. After pulling out a few blocks of dirt, he found what he was looking for: a purple glow.

He dug deeper, revealing the Ender shards that had been linked to her chains.

Steve Alexander looked thoughtfully at the shards for a moment, then lifted one and struck it against a wall. With one hit, it knocked several blocks out of the wall. "Amazing!" he said. "So powerful! That must be why she was chained with these shards! But where did they come from? And also . . ."

He looked into the darkness of the mineshaft, then retraced his steps. Into the portal room he went, stopping in front of the End portal.

"She didn't want to talk about this portal," he mused. "I wonder where it leads. If those who imprisoned the Ender Dragon chose this cave, then the portal inside this cave must be dangerous too . . ."

I could see his mind working, thinking, planning. "A place to trap a dragon . . ." he whispered.

At dawn Steve Alexander made his way out of the bushes toward his home, with Wolf at his side. The night had been long, too long to be natural. He'd spent hours avoiding and fighting armed skeletons and other mobs that had been after him, barely saving himself each time.

As he reached his home, he froze, realizing he was

still not safe. His house was surrounded by armed skel-etons, all standing in the building's shadows. They were obviously waiting there to grab him and take him back to the Ender Dragon.

He hid behind a tree before they could see him. "It's no good," he whispered to Wolf. "If I could get inside my home, I could find more supplies. I can't do this alone, but there's no place in the Overworld that's safe now—and no one in the Overworld I can still trust."

Then his own words gave him an idea.

"The Nether!" he said. He ran to a shed some ways behind his home and threw the doors open. A Nether portal was sitting there, glowing purple in the middle. I understood what he was thinking: if he couldn't find help in this world, then maybe he could find it in another.

Down in the Nether, he assembled a makeshift crafting table and tried making something out of the Ender crystal shards, but nothing seemed to work. And with only hostile mobs around him, he had to keep searching.

He began hauling blocks, trying different objects to construct what looked like portals. "Come on, come on," he begged under his breath. Each attempt failed.

Finally, frustrated, Steve Alexander threw his fist against the blocks on his latest failed portal. "Are there no worlds left?" he cried. "Is there no help?"

Then he noticed Wolf was whimpering and paw-ing at something. He moved some blocks out of the way to see what the dog was so interested in. What he uncovered looked like a new set of rocks, unlike any of those he'd worked with before.

I sucked in a deep breath.

I knew those rocks. Those secret rocks barely anyone in the Overworld knew about. Those were the rocks needed to make a portal to Earth.

CHAPTER 15

STEVE ALEXANDER HAD BEEN THROUGH A LOT IN the past twelve hours, but nothing could prepare him for his first step into this new realm. Mountains, trees, ground—everything was the same, yet everything was so wrong. Instead of being their proper blocky shapes, the mountains, trees, and ground all carved and curved however they wanted to.

And then an Earth woman attacked him.

"It's Maya!" Maison squealed, thrilled. We'd read all about Maya in Steve Alexander's enchanted book. Now we watched their first meeting unfold in real life. At first she thought he was a monster, but when she realized he was human too, she backed off and invited him to come visit her people.

The village she took him to didn't look like any town I'd ever seen on Earth. The villagers were making their own food over open fires and using stone tools instead of their phones. I kind of liked it. The close-to-nature feeling reminded me more of how we lived in the Overworld.

Yancy stared at them, fascinated. "It looks like a hunter-gatherer society! Holy cow, we are way back in time!"

Steve Alexander helped Maya get food for her people, and then the two of them sat and talked. She listened while he told her the whole story of the Ender Dragon. Then she touched the purple crystals he still held.

"And you think this will defeat her?" she asked.

"I think I can make them into a sword," he said. "These shards have clearly been enchanted, and I want to try new enchantments on my weapons, so Jean won't already know how to defend herself against them. I mean"—he cringed—"the Ender Dragon. I guess there never was any Jean."

Maya put her hand on his shoulder. "You have lost much by no longer believing in your friend."

"I don't believe in friends, period," he said.

She looked stern. "How can you say that? We must have friendships, or we can't accomplish anything."

"If I can't trust someone I believed in for years, how can I trust anyone?" he asked sadly.

This time Maya grabbed him by the shoulders and made him look directly into her eyes. "You must believe not everyone is like that. Because even though we just met, I will give you reason to believe in me. I will not sit back and let another suffer when I can help it. We will fight this dragon."

"Ooh, I like her," Alex cut in.

"What do you need from me?" Maya demanded.

"I need your protection while I experiment with enchantments and weapons," he said. "And I want your help putting together an enchanted book I need to write, in case future generations also need to know how to defeat her. And when . . . if . . . I can chase her into that strange portal, into the new land I am going to call the End, I will leave the weapon I create for you to hide. I have never been to the End before, and I don't know what awaits me there. I don't know if there will be a way back, like there is with the Nether portal."

The seriousness of their mission hung in the air between them. Then Maya asked, "Are you sure you are ready to do this?"

"I have to be," he said. "The Ender Dragon was right when she said I was mostly acting heroic because I enjoyed the praise. A truly heroic person does the right thing even if no one will ever know about it. They do the right thing, no matter how dangerous, because it needs to be done. I brought the Ender Dragon into my world—it's my responsibility to take her out of it. If I'm hated forever for unleashing her, so be it. As long as I can end this, I don't care what people call me."

"You are ready," she agreed.

CHAPTER 16

SUDDENLY THE LIGHT SURROUNDED US, AND WE flashed back to where the Ender Dragon and her servants were gathered.

"What do you mean, you still haven't found him?" the Ender Dragon raged.

Mick and Drake trembled in front of her. "Please, have mercy!" Mick said. "The mobs have been searching every corner of the Overworld!"

"It's been a week!" she said. "He should have been found by now!"

"We have his house surrounded," Drake said. "If he returns home, we'll nab him!"

She looked down her snout at both of them for a long moment, then raked her claws in fury across the wall of the jungle temple. Mick and Drake clutched each other and fell to their knees.

"Did it not cross your mind that he's not in the Overworld?" she roared at them.

"He has to be in the Overworld!" Mick said.

"Yeah, where else would he be?" Drake said.

Just then, an arrow flew past the Ender Dragon's head and hit the wall behind her. There was a piece of paper stuck to the arrow, like a note.

The Ender Dragon ripped the arrow loose, letting the paper fall to the floor. It landed by Drake's feet. "What does it say?" she demanded.

Shakily, Drake picked it up. "'I'm at the place where we first met,'" he read. "'Come and get me. S-A.'" He looked at Mick, confused. "Who's S-A?"

"That's Steve Alexander," Mick hissed back. Then he said, with less confidence, "I think."

A cruelly amused smile crawled over the Ender Dragon's mouth. "So he's back," she said. To Mick and Drake, she ordered, "You stay here and watch the jungle temple. I will take care of Steve Alexander. If anything bad happens to the temple while I'm gone, I will hold both of you responsible."

They gave her big nods. But when she flew out into the day, they lay down on the floor as if they hadn't slept all week.

"Wow, I thought she'd never go," Drake said.

"She's always so serious," Mick said.

"Why do you think Steve Alexander said, 'Come and get me'?" Drake asked. "He's been hiding for so long, I didn't think he wanted to be found."

"He was always weird," Mick said. "Let's get some shut-eye."

They both closed their eyes. But they reopened them a moment later when they heard violent shouting outside, as if an angry crowd had gathered.

Drake ran to the window and peered down.

"What is it, Drake?" Mick called.

Drake couldn't look away. "We're done for, Mick!"

An entire army of Overworld soldiers was at the jungle temple doorsteps. At the front of the army was a woman—an Earth woman—with a sword. Maya!

"Charge!" Maya commanded as the army burst through the doors.

Mick and Drake ran to the front of the temple, holding their large wooden swords high. As soon as they got there and saw the sheer number of people, they stopped in their tracks.

"You!" Drake pointed at Maya. "Strange-looking lady! What are you doing here?"

"Completing my mission," she said. She hit something on the wall and disappeared before their eyes. A secret tunnel slid her down through the building, dropping her on her feet in the dungeon. All the prisoners in their cells looked up, amazed.

Maya struck the switch on the wall that unlocked all the cells. "I'm here as a friend of Steve Alexander!" she called. "Everyone, grab a weapon and follow me!"

The villager soldiers who had come with Maya

were already breaking into the dungeon from above, handing extra weapons to the newly freed people.

Maya turned to run back upstairs, only to be stopped by a hand on her arm. She looked and saw Steve Alexander's wife.

"How is Steve Alexander?" his wife exclaimed.

Steve Alexander must have told Maya about his family after we'd flashed away, because Maya didn't ask who this woman was and why she cared. "He is preparing to battle the Ender Dragon," she said. "He told me the layout of the temple so we could take it back."

"What?" Mayor Pandra was horrified. "He can't possibly be thinking of facing the Ender Dragon alone!"

CHAPTER 17

LIGHT ROSE UP AROUND US AGAIN, AND SUDDENLY my friends and I were back in the mineshaft where Steve Alexander had first met the Ender Dragon.

The Ender Dragon slowly trudged into the dark belly of the mineshaft. Her violet eyes narrowed in on Steve Alexander and Wolf as she approached.

In Steve Alexander's hands, a purple sword glistened. Wolf let out a low growl.

"Recognize something?" Steve Alexander asked. "These are the crystals used to chain you before. They were looped in with the chains, but I took out just the crystals for this sword. And I enchanted it."

"Am I supposed to be scared?" she mocked. "As great an inventor as you are, you have never before created a weapon that could stop me."

He dove at her with the sword. She dodged. It was

clearly hard for her to move in this tight, cramped space, but she looked pretty confident in herself.

"I'm surprised you're fighting me right now," she went on. "Don't you need cheering crowds to get anything done?"

"I'm surprised you left the jungle temple for one man in a mineshaft, even though you have all these mobs working for you," he shot back. "Couldn't you have just sent one of your servants to fight me? An armed skeleton, or . . . Drake or Mick?"

She chuckled. "Drake and Mick are the perfect sort of people: they'll follow any fad and they know I'm always right."

"Then how do you think they're doing guarding your jungle temple?" he smirked.

Shouts and screams were echoing into the mineshaft from the entrance behind the Ender Dragon. For the first time, she looked frazzled. Suddenly, Drake burst into the mineshaft, out of breath, and grabbed a wall to steady himself.

"What are you doing here?" she demanded.

"We've lost the jungle temple!" he panted. "The villagers took it back and freed all the prisoners! Some weird-looking lady was leading them, and she knew all the secret passageways! We didn't stand a chance!"

There was a low rumbling sound, like thunder. It took me a second to realize it was the sound of the Ender Dragon growling from deep in her throat. She slashed out with her front paw, knocking Drake across the mineshaft. For a few seconds it looked like he flew. Then he hit another wall, coughing. He was going to be okay, but that was a major blow!

Furious, the Ender Dragon turned back on Steve Alexander. I'd never seen her look scarier than she did right then. Her body looked like an enormous, hulking shadow, barely contained in the tunnel, her fiery purple eyes blazing in the darkness like curses.

Steve Alexander stood his ground, sword out, daring her with his posture. She lunged forward, her fangs showing, trying to bite him. She was so big she could have eaten him for dinner, but when her mouth was just about to close on him, he struck with his sword. The blow was harsher than she expected, knocking her back.

He took this opportunity to strike her again, knocking her back once more. Suddenly I understood what he was doing: he was trying to push her into the room with the End portal!

Her tail swung out and caught his feet, tripping him. Steve Alexander fell to the ground, barely managing to hold on to his sword. By the time he stood back up, the Ender Dragon had stepped farther back and out of his reach.

"That weapon is more dangerous than it looks; I'll give you credit for that," she said. "But that doesn't mean it will defeat me. I still have my army of mobs, and it's dark down here."

As she said it, armed skeletons and Endermen began to spawn in the dark passageway. First it was only Steve Alexander, the Ender Dragon, and Drake, but in moments monsters surrounded them in the darkness, hissing and spitting. Wolf began attacking to keep the mobs away from his master. Still, he could only do so much.

"In here!" a voice called from outside. This wiped the smug smile off the Ender Dragon's face. As the mobs were all closing in on Steve Alexander, a woman burst into the mineshaft, holding a torch and a diamond sword. She was followed by more villagers with weapons.

"Maya!" Steve Alexander cried, relieved.

"I told you I'd give you a reason to believe in friends again!" Maya said, slashing back at an armed skeleton with her sword.

"No matter what happens, I will never forget you, Maya!" he shouted back.

The Ender Dragon looked around the scene frantically. The villagers were taking care of all the mobs, freeing up Steve Alexander to fight her. And suddenly Steve Alexander's wife and son were beside him! He looked relieved to see them safe and out of their dungeon cells.

Steve Alexander got a brief second to hug and whisper something to his family. Then he turned his hard eyes back on the Ender Dragon and strode toward her, no hesitation in his step. He wasn't a stammering, nervous wreck anymore. He had the look of a man on a mission who would not be stopped.

He looked like a hero.

The Ender Dragon took a step back. She shot purple fireballs out of her mouth in every direction, not caring whether they hit villagers or mobs. The villagers would be okay, but the affected mobs were easily finished off by the non-affected villagers. Steve Alexander easily dodged the fireballs' paths, avoiding them completely. He stood before his former best friend, his sword out.

"Enough!" he said. "This is between you and me. It's time to end this."

CHAPTER 18

WITH MOBS AND VILLAGERS STILL FIGHTING in the background, Steve Alexander and the Ender Dragon lunged for each other. He slashed his sword while she kept trying to blast him, each barely dodging the other's attack. They were on pretty even footing, which had to worry the Ender Dragon. With their size difference, she should have easily been in control. But Steve Alexander was matching her for everything she had, and she couldn't move much in the mineshaft's tunnels. As their fight raged on, he succeeded in pushing her back into the portal room.

I could barely tear my eyes away for a second. Destiny was biting her fingernails. Alex looked ready to join the battle if only she could.

I didn't know how the stalemate would break. Then the Ender Dragon gained a slight advantage.

Her tail struck out, hitting up against Maya, Mayor Pandra, and the boy Steve, who were all standing near one another. She slammed them all back against the wall, keeping them caught there behind her tail. The three of them struggled but couldn't break free.

"No!" Steve Alexander cried.

"You see, even now you still have weaknesses," the Ender Dragon said. "That's why you turned down my offer for power, and that's why you'd never make a good ruler. If you really want to be number one, you can only look out for yourself. If anyone else gets in the way, no matter how much you think you care about them, you must let them go."

"Release them and fight me!" he shouted.

She shook her head. "They are my prisoners. Bow to me and I will release them. Fight me, and I will make you all very sorry."

Oh no! I thought. My heart was pounding so hard it hurt. I itched to defend Steve Alexander. I felt so helpless, only being able to watch. All the legends I knew about Steve Alexander had never mentioned any of this!

He was gasping for breath, and his eyes were darting around as he tried to figure out what to do. The Ender Dragon waited, enjoying her advantage.

"You're right that Drake and Mick are fools," she said. "But you are so much more clever. I want you at my side again. Think about all our nights together, our battles. Think of all the statues of us. We will go down in history together, you and I. We can go down as mortal enemies, or we can go down in the history books as a team."

"Sorry, not falling for it," he said. "I've learned a lot since I met you, Jean." The use of her old name made the Ender Dragon cringe and close her eyes. He went on, "I learned about betrayal, about greed, about not being able to believe that everything is as it first appears. I have you to thank for those lessons. But that's not all. By knowing you, I also learned about true friendship, about those who will help you even if it doesn't involve them, those who think for themselves, and those who will stand up when they see something is wrong."

The Ender Dragon let out a shriek. I saw that Maya had somehow pulled her sword arm out from under the dragon's tail and struck with all her might. This made the Ender Dragon's tail recoil, releasing her prisoners.

It also gave Steve Alexander the perfect opportunity. He leaped forward, his sword raised. It struck the Ender Dragon in the chest, forcing her back. Another strike! She stepped back again, her legs unsteady. Her feet were touching the steps that led to the End portal. They'd almost made it!

Steve Alexander drew back his sword arm. I held my breath. The sword forced the Ender Dragon back even more, her back feet clumsily slipping into the portal. She tried to rear up and free herself, but he didn't give her the chance. He vaulted toward her, and for a second it looked like Steve Alexander was flying, his feet off the ground, his sword held high. Wolf was leaping with him. There was an explosion of light as his sword struck the dragon and he forced her all the way into the portal. Then dragon, man, and dog all fell through the portal and were gone. The purple sword dropped to the floor of the mineshaft, glinting.

CHAPTER 19

THE PEOPLE OF THE OVERWORLD WERE ALL CRYing out and rubbing their eyes. Maya approached the fallen sword and picked it up, holding it close to her.

Drake, clutching his side, inched forward. "Where'd Steve Alexander go? What happened?"

Maya turned on him fiercely. "He's in the End!" she shouted. "He told me he didn't know if he could ever escape it, but that he would go there if he had to to stop the Ender Dragon."

The people took this in, dazed. They had looks that said they would never do what he did, but they were grateful he'd had the guts to do it.

"I shouldn't have made so much fun of him before," said a voice. A hooded man in the crowd was speaking. I recognized him from an earlier scene—he was the man who had asked Drake and Mick to give him dirt on Steve Alexander. "I thought he only fought monsters for glory, but if he did this . . . he's a hero."

Maya looked at the man for a long time. "Is that how you'll remember him?"

"Yes!" the man insisted. "He was the greatest hero the Overworld has ever seen! He saved all of us!"

"And so the legend is born," someone whispered next to me. It was Yancy, who looked as stunned as I was by the true story of what had happened. I could understand. I was feeling shaky, like I needed to sit down.

Maya turned and looked at the crowd. "What Steve Alexander had in him, and what he chose to do, is a possibility for all of us," she shouted. "He was not perfect. But when he realized the true threat of the Ender Dragon, he didn't care what happened to him, so long as she was stopped. It's easy to show bravery when everyone around you is being brave. It is much scarier and more noble to show bravery when no one else will."

There was another light, and I wondered what were we going to be shown now. This experience had answered so many questions, but I still had a ton! I didn't hate Steve Alexander or think he was a liar anymore. I had wanted to believe he was perfect, and I knew Maya was right when she said he wasn't. But seeing him for who he really was, mistakes and all, had kind of made me like him even more. He felt more real now than he had as a statue meant to symbolize everything that is good. I'd fought some pretty scary things in my life, though nothing on the scale of what Steve Alexander had defeated. Could I ever be like him?

I thought we were going to see another scene, but when the light cleared this time and I blinked, we were back in Maison's bedroom. The book was no longer glowing. It looked like a normal book, and my friends standing around me in Maison's room made up a normal scene. Except we were all blinking and overwhelmed.

"Wait, I still have questions!" Maison cried. "Did Steve Alexander find a way to get out of the End? Did he return home?"

"I feel so bad for him going into the End like that," Destiny said. I could see that she'd really bitten her nails down to the quick during our journey through time. "Just him, his dog, and the Ender Dragon—forever?"

"I'm sure he got out," Alex said. "You saw how smart he was, and that vision was only about stuff happening around the battle against the Ender Dragon."

We all had seen how smart he was, though I didn't know if that meant anything when it came to the End. Still, I hoped Alex was right!

"We still have a big, big problem," Yancy pointed out. "None of that helped us find the Ender crystal shard. And if we don't find that, we're still done for."

CHAPTER 20

THEN THERE WAS A KNOCK ON THE DOOR. MAI-
son jumped. We all looked at each other, horrified.

Despite all of the adventures we'd shared, Maison's
mom still didn't know about Alex, me, or the *Minecraft*
world. My dad knew about our adventures in different
worlds, and I'd always wondered how Maison kept all
our shared experiences from her mom. It sure seemed
like her mom should be asking more questions.

"Hide!" Maison whispered to Alex and me. She
called out, "Just a second, Mom!"

The door opened anyway. Alex and I froze, caught
in Maison's mom's stare. She'd seen us once before,
but that was when most people were brainwashed by
Herobrine, so she hadn't realized that we were from
another world. What was she going to say now?

I thought Maison's mom might flip out or scream

or tell someone to call the police. Instead she smiled at us, and said, "It's about time we all met."

"Mom?" Maison said, unbelieving.

"Oh, be serious," her mom said, sitting down on the edge of the bed casually, as though she met people from a different world every day. What was going on here? "Zombies tear up my house, Maison stops a monster takeover at her middle school . . . You didn't think I had any idea of what my own daughter was doing?"

My mouth was hanging open. I didn't know how to close it right then.

"Mom?" Maison said again, still unable to believe it.

Maison's mom shook hands with Alex and me, which was a little weird, given that she has fingers and we don't.

"Wait, hold on," Yancy said. "You don't find this odd at all?"

She smiled at Yancy as if he were being cute. But Yancy wasn't someone who acted cute.

"No, not at all," she said. "It's about time we have a talk, though, Maison. In this family, for many generations, we have given a special gift to our daughters on their twelfth birthdays. I know it's still a few days away, but I think it is time."

She reached into her pocket and pulled out something glowing.

CHAPTER 21

MAISON GASPED AS THE PURPLE GLOW LIT UP her face. The crystal shard was hanging on a chain, like a necklace. But it was an Ender crystal shard, no doubt about it.

"How . . . ?" was all Maison could get out.

"We have known about the Overworld for thousands of years," her mom said. "When our ancestor, Maya, had a daughter, she gave this crystal to her on her twelfth birthday. She told her daughter then about the adventures she had shared with Steve Alexander. She vowed that the crystal would always remain in her family, in case the Ender Dragon was ever freed and needed to be stopped again."

"Maya is . . . my ancestor?" Maison's eyes were brimming with emotion as she heard this.

"You mean it?" I looked wildly back and forth between Maison and her mom. "Our families go way back!"

"Yes," Maison's mom said. "It is your destiny to be together as friends and allies. And it is your destiny to fight the dragon once more."

Yancy was staring at the Ender crystal, astonished. "So that was what the clue meant? Find the Earth woman. Find Maison!"

Maison was holding the Ender crystal in her hand like the most precious gift. Her eyes still had that trembling look.

"Does that mean we're not part of this destiny?" Destiny asked. "Our family doesn't have any history like that."

"As far as we know," Yancy put in. "Until two minutes ago, we didn't know Maison had this ancestry, either."

"Of course it is still part of your destiny," Maison's mom said. "You have chosen this path in all your past adventures, and through your determination to stop the Ender Dragon now. It doesn't matter where you came from—your choices are noble choices, and you are just as much a part of the fight as Maison."

Wow, I thought. She even talked a bit like Maya.

Maison was kind of laughing and choking at the same time, still staring at the Ender crystal. "I can't believe it! I just can't . . ."

"It was your connection to Maya that must have led you to the stones you needed to make the Earth portal," Maison's mom said. She tucked a stray hair behind Maison's ear. "I am so glad I can finally share all of this with you."

"Does this mean you'll also help us in the battle against the Ender Dragon?" Yancy asked.

"Of course," Maison's mom said. "When I was twelve, I was told it might someday be my duty. I am ready."

There was a lot of excited talking and planning after that. We needed to get this crystal shard back to my house and show it to Dad, and then we could combine it with the other crystal shards and make a sword, like Steve Alexander had done. With all the crystal shards safely in our hands and out of the grasp of the Ender Dragon, we actually stood a chance of defeating her!

Suddenly, I could feel something stirring behind me.

I whirled. Two Endermen had stepped through Maison's computer, right into her bedroom!

"Maison!" I cried.

It all happened so fast. The Endermen teleported right over to Maison, grabbing her by each arm. Alex drew back her arrows and sent them flying, but it was too late. I heard Maison let out a shriek, I heard the arrows fly—and then Maison and the Endermen were gone!

"No!" I cried, jumping up. "How did they get here?"

"The Ender Dragon's power must have grown stronger!" Yancy exclaimed. "She's able to transport her mobs to Earth!"

"Maison!" her mom shouted frantically, running to the computer. "Maison, where are you?"

I knew better than to look in this room. The Endermen were long gone—and they had Maison, and the last of the Ender crystal.

"Through the portal!" I shouted. "Maybe we can find her on the other side!"

I dove through the computer screen.

Everything went green, blue, and red, and then I fell out the other end, landing safely in the Overworld. I was back in my house, and it was all still in one piece. Dad was standing there, looking at me in concern. I saw he had grabbed his diamond sword.

"Stevie!" he said. "I was just about to go get you! There were Endermen in the house, even though the whole place is blocked off!"

I ran past him and out the door. The entire sky was darkening, and not with clouds. With night. And it was hours before it would normally get dark! A cold, terrifying wind arose, shaking the trees.

"Maison!" I called. Did the Endermen teleport back to where they'd come from? If they'd somehow used the portal here, they might still be nearby! But my cries only hit the wind, and remained unanswered.

The door of my house burst open behind me, and Alex, Destiny, Yancy, and Maison's mom ran through it. Dad was right behind, sword up. He didn't even ask Maison's mom who she was.

"How long has the sky been like this?" Yancy asked in a panicked voice.

"It started minutes ago," Dad said. "Then two Endermen appeared."

"Maison!" I cried again. The wind was screaming even louder than I was. Since when did we get winds like this in the Overworld?

There was a strange object floating in the sky, almost like a bank of green clouds. But when I looked at it, I saw it was something else. Something so much worse. My whole body trembled.

It was an End portal. An End portal in the sky.

Suddenly the portal seemed to explode in white light. We all covered our eyes with our arms, protecting ourselves. And then I slowly let my arm drop, dreading what I would see.

"At last," said a voice in the sky.

There she was, her enormous body hovering in the dark skies above me, her purple eyes aflame, her days of imprisonment behind her.

The Ender Dragon was free!

DO YOU LIKE FICTION FOR MINECRAFTERS?

Read the rest of the Unofficial Overworld Heroes Adventure series to find out what happens to Stevie ar the Overworld Heroes!

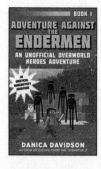

Adventure Against the Endermen
DANICA DAVIDSON

Mysteries of the Overworld
DANICA DAVIDSON

Danger in the Jungle Temple
DANICA DAVIDSON

Clash in the Underwater World
DANICA DAVIDSON

The Last of the Ender Crystal
DANICA DAVIDSON

Return of the Ender Dragon
DANICA DAVIDSON

Available wherever books are sold!